# SHARON CREECH

# Fishing in the Air

## PICTURES BY
## CHRIS RASCHKA

JOANNA COTLER BOOKS
*An Imprint of* HarperCollins*Publishers*

Fishing in the Air
Text copyright © 2000 by Sharon Creech
Illustrations copyright © 2000 by Chris Raschka
Manufactured in China. All rights reserved.

For information address HarperCollins
Children's Books, a division of HarperCollins
Publishers, 10 East 53rd Street,
New York, NY 10022.
www.harperchildrens.com

Library of Congress Cataloging-in-Publication Data
Creech, Sharon.
   Fishing in the air / by Sharon Creech ; pictures by Chris Raschka.
      p.      cm.
   "Joanna Cotler books."
   Summary: A young boy and his father go on a fishing trip and
discover the power of imagination.
   ISBN 0-06-028111-1. — ISBN 0-06-028112-X (lib. bdg.)
   ISBN 0-06-051606-2 (pbk.)
   [1. Father and son—Fiction.   2. Fishing—Fiction.
3. Imagination—Fiction.]   I. Raschka, Christopher, ill.   II. Title.
PZ7.C8615Fi   2000                                    99-35538
[E]—dc21                                              CIP
                                                      AC

Typography by Alicia Mikles
10 11 12 13 SCP 10 9 8 7 6
❖

*For my fishing nieces:*

*Annie, Sandra Kay, and Mary Rose*

—S.C.

*For Lydie and for Ingo*

—C.R.

One Saturday, when I was young, my father and I left the house early in the morning, when it was still blue-black outside. The grass left wet marks on our shoes. In the backyard, under stones, we dug up crawly worms and laid them in a can with lumps of damp dirt.

Into the trunk we put two poles and the can of worms and a sack of sandwiches and a thermos of water.

"We're going on a journey," my father said. "To a secret place. We'll catch the air! We'll catch the breeze!"

We slipped into the car and closed the doors quietly and off we went.

"Look at those streetlamps," my father said, "glowing like tiny moons all in a row."

And the lamps which had been lamps became,
in an instant, tiny moons all in a row.

We drove and drove along the road, until we came to a narrow lane. We bumped along, along, along the winding lane.

"Those trees," my father said, "don't they look like tall green soldiers standing at attention?"

And the trees which had been trees became, in an instant, tall green soldiers standing at attention.

We were going on a journey. To a secret place. We'd catch the air! We'd catch the breeze!

When we stopped, my father said, "Ah, what a sky! White white clouds and a golden sun and bubbles of breeze and birds singing their songs like little angels."

And the birds which had been birds became, in an instant, little angels singing their songs.

"I'd like to take those clouds, that sun, those bubbles of breeze, and those angel birds home with me," my father said. He took my hand and said, "I smell a river!"

I sniffed. I smelled it too.

We took our poles and our food,
and we ducked through the trees. And
there, beyond the trees, was the river.

"Oh, I love a clear, cool river," my
father said, "such a clear, cool river,
rolling along over sandy-colored stones.
I'd like to take that river home."

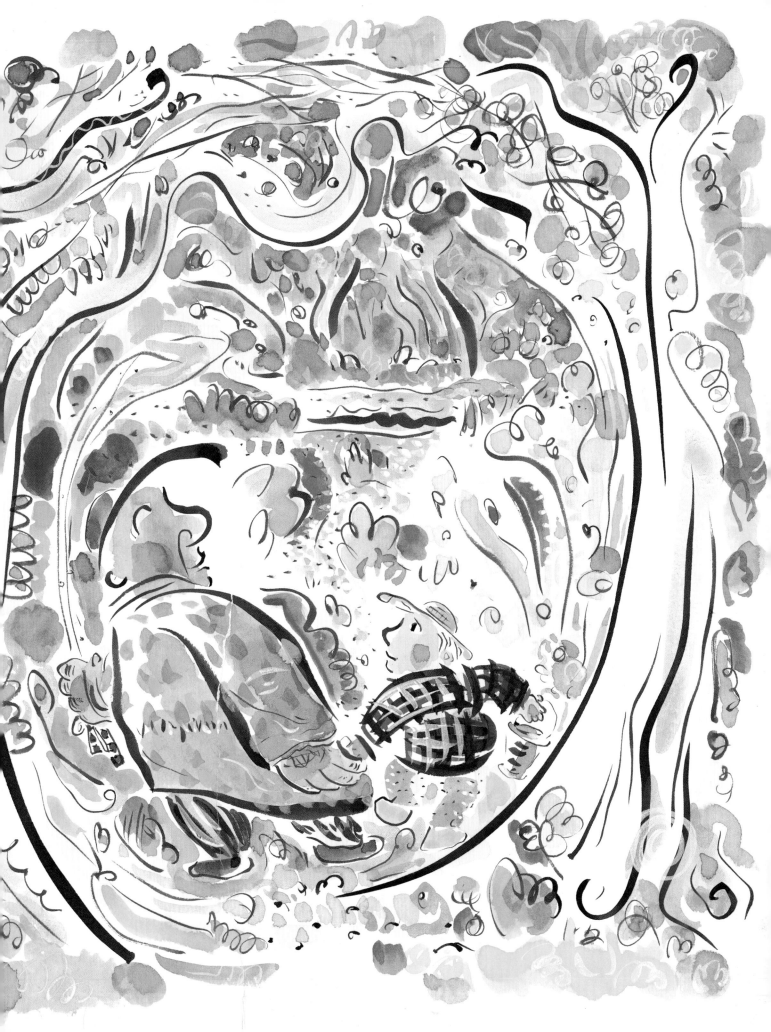

My father baited his hook and cast his line into the water.

"When I was a boy," my father said, "I caught the air, I caught the breeze, and I took them home with me."

My line had no hook, only a blue feather midway down the line and a red and white bobber near the end. I cast the line high above my head.

"And where did you live when you were
a boy?" I asked.

"In a small house," he said.

I looked at my father, a big man. "What was it like, your house?" I asked. "The house you lived in when you were a boy?"

He closed his eyes. "It was a small gray house
with a crooked porch and tiny windows and a
red roof. It looked like a little box with a red hat."

I cast my line, and it flew high into the air.
I caught a bubble of breeze.

"What was it like outside your house, the house
you lived in when you were a boy?" I asked.

"There were green fields around it, rolling
green fields with bright red flowers here and there
like floating rubies, and all around the fields
were trees, tall green green trees," my father said.

I reeled in my line and cast again. High, high
it flew. I caught a sliver of sky.

"And what was beyond the trees?" I asked.
"Beyond those trees that were around the fields
that were around the house you lived in as a boy?"

"There was a river, clear and cool, that rippled
over stones," my father said, "and there I learned
to fish."

I reeled in my line. I cast it high and far, and it sailed into the air, its blue feather waving in the breeze. I caught a slice of yellow sun.

"And," I asked, "who taught you how to fish in that clear, cool river beyond the trees around the green fields around the gray house you lived in when you were a boy?"

"Ah," he said, with his eyes closed tightly, "it was my father. My father taught me how to fish in the clear, cool river."

My bobber bounced
on the water, and the blue
feather waved in the air.
I reeled it in and cast again and
caught a white white cloud.

"Oh, where is that house?" my
father said. "And where are those
fields and that river and that father
and that boy?"

I reeled in my line. I cast it higher
and farther, and it sailed lazily
through the air. And this time I
caught it all.

I caught a bubble of breeze
and a sliver of sky and a slice of
yellow sun and a small gray house
with a crooked porch and tiny windows
and a red roof and rolling green fields
with red flowers waving and tall green
green trees and a river rippling
cool and clear.

"Oh," my father said again.
"Where is that father
and that boy?"
I reeled in my line.
"Right here," I said,
and he turned to look at me,
as I cast my line again
so high, so far.

And at the end of the day, after we'd put our fishing poles back into the trunk and set off down the winding lane, he said, "We've been on a journey. To a secret place. We caught the air! We caught the breeze!"

And we also caught a small gray house
with a crooked porch and tiny windows
and a red roof and rolling green fields
with red flowers waving and tall green
green trees and a river rippling
cool and clear.

And we caught a father,
and we caught a boy,
who learned to fish.